The Purple Pussycat

by Margaret Hillert

Illustrated by Krystyna Stasiak

DEAR CAREGIVER,

The *Beginning-to-Read* series is a carefully written collection of classic readers you may remember from your own childhood. Each book features text comprised of common sight words to provide your child ample practice reading the words that appear most frequently in written text. The many additional details in the pictures enhance the story and offer the opportunity for you to help your child expand oral language and develop comprehension.

Begin by reading the story to your child, followed by letting him or her read familiar words and soon your child will be able to read the story independently. At each step of the way, be sure to praise your reader's efforts to build his or her confidence as an independent reader. Discuss the pictures and encourage your child to make connections between the story and his or her own life. At the end of the story, you will find reading activities and a word list that will help your child practice and strengthen beginning reading skills.

Above all, the most important part of the reading experience is to have fun and enjoy it!

Shannon Cannon

Shannon Cannon,
Literacy Consultant

For Mama, who dreamed him— M.H.

Norwood House Press • P.O. Box 316598 • Chicago, Illinois 60631
For more information about Norwood House Press please visit our website at
www.norwoodhousepress.com or call 866-565-2900.

LIBRARY OF CONGRESS CATALOGING-IN-PUBLICATION DATA
Hillert, Margaret.
 The purple pussycat / by Margaret Hillert; illustrated by Krystyna
Stasiak. — Rev. and expanded library ed.
 p. cm. — (A beginning-to-read book)
 Summary: A stuffed pussycat comes to life at night and sets out to explore
the world. Includes reading activities.
 ISBN-13: 978-1-59953-044-4 (library binding : alk. paper)
 ISBN-10: 1-59953-044-9 (library binding : alk. paper)
 [1. Toys—Fiction. 2. Animals—Fiction.] I. Stasiak, Krystyna, ill. II.
Title. III. Series: Hillert, Margaret. Beginning to read series. Easy
stories.
 PZ7.H558Pu 2007
 [E]—dc22   2006007889

We can not play now.
We have work to do.
Can you help me?

Now we can go.
Come with me.
I want you to come.

Here we are.
I like you here with me.
This is good.

I want to go out.
I will jump down.
Here I go.

You can play here.
You can have fun.
But I will go away.
You can not come with me.

Out, out I go.
Out to see what I can see.
This is fun.

Oh, look up.
Look up, up, up.
How big it is!
It is pretty.
I like it.

And see what is here.
Look at this.
One, two, three little ones.

The little ones jump.
The little ones run.
The little ones play.

I can run and jump, too.
I can play.
I like it out here.

Oh, oh.
What is this?
It looks like me.
It runs and jumps, too.
I can make it run.
What fun!

17

Something is up here.
What is it?
What is it?

Oh, I see you now.
You are big.
Who are you?
Who? Who?

And here is something little.
I see you, too.
You will have to run.

Run away, little one.
Run, run, run.
Something will get you.

Now I will go here.
What will I find here?
What will I see now?

I see you work.
I see what you have.
You will eat it.

Away I go.
Away I go
to see what I can see.

Oh, my.
Look at this.
What a good mother this is.

Here I am.
And in I go.
In, in, in.

You are here with me,
but we can get up now.
Get up. Get up.
Come out and play with me.

READING REINFORCEMENT

The following activities support the findings of the National Reading Panel that determined the most effective components for reading instruction are: Phonemic Awareness, Phonics, Vocabulary, Fluency, and Text Comprehension.

Phonemic Awareness: The /p/ sound

Oddity Task: Say the /**p**/ sound for your child. Ask your child to say the word that doesn't have the /**p**/ sound in the following word groups:

pat, tap, mat	park, mark, pack	set, pet, step
peach, reach, pea	met, pet, up	spot, top, ten
seat, sleep, keep	mark, spark, speck	

Phonics: The letter Pp

1. Demonstrate how to form the letters **P** and **p** for your child.

2. Have your child practice writing **P** and **p** at least three times each.

3. Ask your child to point to the words in the book that have the letter **p** in them.

4. Write down the following words and ask your child to circle the letter **p** in each word:

play	help	pretty	puppy
jump	pop	skip	nap
peep	pan	pepper	stamp

Vocabulary: Opposites

1. The story features the concepts of big and little. Discuss opposites and ask your child to name the opposites of the following:

in (out)	up (down)	play (work)	good (bad)
hard (soft)	happy (sad)	tall (short)	clean (dirty)
quiet (loud)	old (new)		

2. Write each of the words on separate pieces of paper. Mix the words up and ask your child to put the opposite pairs back together.

Fluency: Choral Reading

1. Reread the story with your child at least two more times while your child tracks the print by running a finger under the words as they are read. Ask your child to read the words he or she knows with you.

2. Reread the story aloud together. Be careful to read at a rate that your child can keep up with.

3. Repeat choral reading and allow your child to be the lead reader and ask him or her to change from a whisper to a loud voice while you follow along and change your voice.

Text Comprehension: Discussion Time

1. Ask your child to retell the sequence of events in the story.

2. To check comprehension, ask your child the following questions:

- What are the little animals that jump, run and play in the story?

- What does the Purple Pussycat see on page 16?

- Why does the Purple Pussycat tell the mouse to run away on page 23?

- What does your favorite stuffed animal look like?

- Can you tell a story about an adventure your favorite stuffed animal might have when you're asleep?

The Purple Pussycat uses the 58 words listed below.

This list can be used to practice reading the words that appear in the text.
You may wish to write the words on index cards and use them to help your
child build automatic word recognition. Regular practice with these words
will enhance your child's fluency in reading connected text.

am	find	jump (s)	play	want
and	fun		pretty	we
are		like		what
at	get	little	run (s)	who
away	go	look (s)		will
	good		see	with
big		make	something	work
but	have	me		
	help	mother	the	you
can	here	my	this	
come	how		three	
		not	to	
do	I	now	too	
down	in		two	
	is	oh		
eat	it	one (s)	up	
		out		

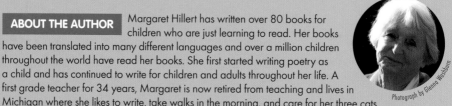

ABOUT THE AUTHOR Margaret Hillert has written over 80 books for
children who are just learning to read. Her books
have been translated into many different languages and over a million children
throughout the world have read her books. She first started writing poetry as
a child and has continued to write for children and adults throughout her life. A
first grade teacher for 34 years, Margaret is now retired from teaching and lives in
Michigan where she likes to write, take walks in the morning, and care for her three cats.

Photograph by Glenna Washburn

ABOUT THE ADVISER Shannon Cannon contributed the activities pages that appear in
this book. Shannon serves as a literacy consultant and provides
staff development to help improve reading instruction. She is a frequent presenter at educational
conferences and workshops. Prior to this she worked as an elementary school teacher and as
president of a curriculum publishing company.